From Your Diary with Love

New Girl Blues

On her tenth birthday,
shy Evie Denham's life
is turned around by a
special present. In the
pages of a beautiful
purple diary lies the
key to her happiness . . .

When her family moves from London to the little town of Crossacre, talented dancer Evie finds it difficult to settle in to her new life. On Evie's birthday, her mysterious neighbour, Mrs Volkov, gives her a beautiful purple velvet diary as a present. But this is no ordinary journal: every time Evie pens an entry and tucks it under her pillow overnight, she discovers the book has written back the following morning with words of guidance. Evie's diary soon becomes her treasured friend, holding the secret to her finding her feet in Crossacre, and giving her the confidence to do what she does best:

dance!

'My favourite bit of this book was when Evie
had her birthday tea at the restaurant'
Jodie, age 7

'I loved it when Evie discovers that
her diary is magical'
Holly, age 9

'The diary is amazing the way it
actually replies to Evie'
Victoria, age 8

'I would love to have a magical friend like this'
Katie, age 9

'I like the fact that this series is magical
because I love magical books'
Lucy, age 9

*We want to hear
what you think about*
From Your Diary
With Love! *Visit*

www.egmont.co.uk/fromyourdiary

*where the magic
continues . . .*

This diary is for you alone,
A secret you must keep,
Each night, tell me your worries,
And then fall sound asleep.

And as the dawn sun wakes you up,
The answer will be here,
Some words to help and guide you,
So you need have no fear.

Evie, please keep me safe and hidden,
For if anyone finds out,
These words will fade, and I'll be gone.
Of this there is no doubt.

And later, when my work is done,
Please don't put me aside.
Pass me on, wish me goodbye,
And someone else I'll guide.

Special thanks to:
Nick Baker, West Jesmond Primary School, Maney Hill
Primary School and Courthouse Junior School

EGMONT
We bring stories to life

New Girl Blues first published in Great Britain 2008
by Egmont UK Limited
239 Kensington High Street, London W8 6SA

Text & illustration © 2008 Egmont UK Ltd
Text by Nick Baker
Illustrations by Mélanie Florain

ISBN 978 1 4052 3949 3

1 3 5 7 9 10 8 6 4 2

A CIP catalogue record for this title is available
from the British Library

Typeset by Avon DataSet Ltd, Bidford on Avon, Warwickshire
Printed and bound in Great Britain by the CPI Group

From Your Diary with Love

New Girl Blues

Laura Baker

Illustrated by Mélanie Florain

EGMONT

The Denham Family

Charlie Denham

He's Evie's cool older brother who has lots of friends at school and loves playing sport, but always finds time to look out for his little sister

Evie Denham

Evie is a shy, quiet girl but with a little help and advice she hopes to make all her dancing dreams come true

Evie's Mum

She's a nurse at the local hospital and is keen for her children to feel at home in Crossacre

Evie's Dad

He's happy to have escaped city life, and when he's not enjoying the quiet surroundings of Crossacre he's running his own Internet business

Josh Denham

He's Evie's little brother. He can be a nosy pest a lot of the time, but he loves Evie really and looks up to her a lot

The Malkova Dance Academy
Students and Staff

Meera Stevens
Evie's friend and a talented artist

Lottie Dean
Thinks she's the star of The Malkova Dance Academy

Mrs Violet Swann
She's the wise principal of the dance academy who her pupils look up to

Jess Whittington
Evie's friend and a hard worker

Dame Malkova

The legendary prima ballerina who founded the academy and who still manages to inspire the students years later

Lauren Davies

Evie's friend and a natural athlete

Miss Connie Swann

She's a beautiful and kind dance teacher who always inspires her students

Matt Shanklin

He's the only boy at the academy and a reluctant dancer

Beth Dickinson

She's Evie's best friend and excellent at modern dance

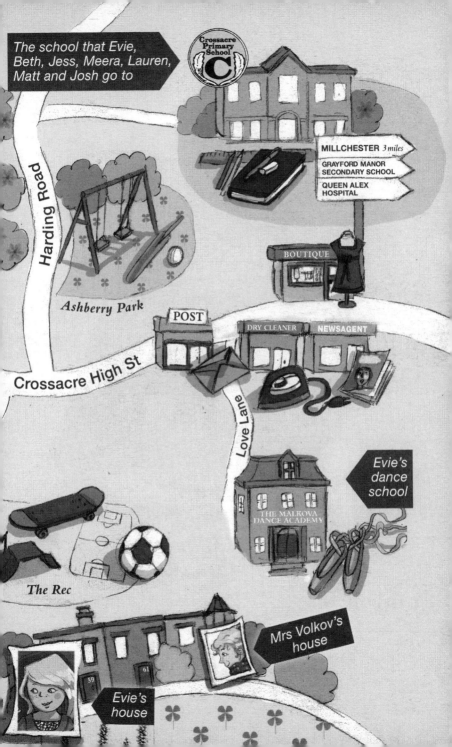

Contents

Chapter One

Late Lunch

Evie sat at her desk doodling in the back of her history book. She added another pretty ballerina to the line dancing round the page and sighed sadly. A whole week had passed since she'd joined Crossacre School, but it felt like she'd *never* fit in.

In the playground on her first morning everyone had crowded around excitedly, and Evie had felt thrilled to be meeting a group of new friends.

'Where are you from?' a girl called Meera asked with a pleasant smile.

Evie started to explain that her family had just moved from London, but suddenly realised that no one was listening. A skinny girl with streaked black hair and long pink nails, obviously the Queen of Cool, had pushed her way to the front of the crowd. She stood with her arms folded and her head tilted to one side.

'So,' she said with a sneer, 'who's your favourite band?'

Everyone fell silent. Evie quavered, knowing that if she gave the wrong name they'd all laugh at her.

'Um, I like lots of different bands –' she began.

'Huh!' sniffed the girl rolling her eyes before

strutting off with a follow-me flick of her head. The others followed or drifted away, leaving Evie standing alone, blinking back the tears that filled her eyes.

'Perhaps you can tell me, Evie?' said Mr Mitchin, 5M's teacher.

Evie jumped and stopped doodling. 'Sorry, sir,' she stammered. 'What did you say?'

Mr Mitchin looked over his half-moon glasses and smiled kindly. 'Could you tell me what this is?' he repeated, holding up something that looked like a doughnut.

Evie shook her head and wished she had been listening.

'It's an Ancient Roman –' began Mr Mitchin, when there was a knock on the door.

'Come in,' called Mr Mitchin, and into the

classroom marched a nurse carrying a large red apple and a glittery plastic lunch box.

Evie cringed – it was Mum, on her way to work at Millchester hospital.

'I'm so sorry to interrupt,' said Mrs Denham, 'but Evie left her lunch at home.'

Evie blushed brighter than the apple and hid her face in her hands.

'Would you please make sure,' continued Mrs Denham, 'that she eats her fruit before her crisps.'

'Ohhh!' groaned Evie and shrank in her chair, wishing she could disappear as Mum turned round and blew her a kiss.

Uproar broke out. Everyone began chattering and laughing; Anthony and Joseph, the class jokers, blew kisses at all the girls; only Beth kept quiet, though Evie didn't notice – she still had her face in her hands.

This is so horrid! she thought. *Why did Mum*

have to come and embarrass me?

'Quiet, please!' said Mr Mitchin with a grin. Even he was chuckling!

'Please, sir,' said Anthony, trying to keep a straight face. 'I feel ill. I think I ate my breakfast cereal before my yoghurt. Do you think I'll survive?'

'Very amusing, Anthony,' said Mr Mitchin. 'Mind you don't starve, though – I see you've left some yoghurt on your chin!'

Anthony laughed and rubbed it away.

Joseph put up his hand. 'Please, sir. You'd better check if Evie's mum cut the crusts off her sandwiches, or she might break her little toothies.'

Before Mr Mitchin could reply a girl with beautiful, big brown eyes called angrily across the room at Joseph, 'Well, I bet Evie wouldn't cry because she's scared of the tooth fairy . . . like *someone* did in year three!'

Everyone laughed and Evie's lunch box was forgotten.

'Thank you for that, Beth,' said Mr Mitchin. 'Now, back to the Ancient Romans . . .'

Evie felt so mixed up that, though she tried, she couldn't concentrate. By the end of the lesson, her line of ballerinas had reached the edge of the page. With a clattering of chairs, everyone charged from the classroom and down the corridor.

Evie couldn't remember where she had to go and rushed after them, terrified of being left behind. They stopped at the gym, where half the girls had already changed for PE. Evie quickly put on her top, shorts and trainers and ran into the hall.

Everyone except her was wearing tracksuit

bottoms! A few girls pointed and sniggered, but the teacher kindly lent her some bottoms from lost property. *Oh*, she thought with a sigh. *Am I always going to be the odd one out?*

After lunch, hoping to thank Beth for standing up for her in history, and longing for an invitation to join in, Evie hung around near a group of girls who were French skipping. No one even noticed her.

Feeling more lonely than ever, Evie swallowed hard. *I wish I was in London with Hannah*, she thought, *huddled in our special place, planning a sleepover and giggling about everything. If only I could go back to my old school and my real home ...*

Chapter Two

An Invitation

Mum had hurried back from her shift at the hospital, fed the cat, emptied the dishwasher, cooked dinner *and* laid the table. She then went into the sitting room where Evie's big brother was watching TV.

'Charlie,' she said, wiping her forehead with the back of her hand. 'Please would you pop upstairs and call Dad for dinner.'

Dad was in his loft office, designing a new web site on his computer. Since the move from London he seemed to spend all his time up there, just popping out like a bunny from a burrow to eat a meal, then disappearing again until bedtime.

Charlie rolled off the sofa and crawled up the stairs.

When they were all sitting at the kitchen table Mum gave Evie a plate of spaghetti smothered with chicken pieces in creamy sauce. 'Here you are, love,' she said. 'It's your favourite!'

'Thanks, Mum,' Evie said quietly.

'I want *my* favourite!' moaned Josh. Evie sighed. Since starting year two at their new school, her little brother had become more annoying than ever. She speared a piece of chicken with her fork – she loved him dearly, but sometimes he made her want to scream . . . arghh!

'It'll be your turn tomorrow, Josh,' said Mum.

'But I *hate* spaghetti!' he yelled.

'Last week you said you loved it!' Mum reminded him.

'Oh, yes,' he said with a grin, and sucked up a long strand that whirled round like a propeller, flicking sauce down his new Chelsea football shirt.

Everyone tucked in except Evie, who picked at her meal and hardly spoke. Mum glanced at Dad and raised her eyebrows.

'Did you know, Josh,' said Charlie with a grin, 'the Chelsea captain said anyone who gets sauce on a team shirt has to give it back.'

'Nooo!' said Josh, gripping his shirt as if the football police might rush in and take it away.

Charlie rubbed his chin and looked up at the ceiling. 'I can't see why they'd bother, actually, considering Chelsea are *completely rubbish*!'

'No, they're not! They're the best!' Josh shouted.

'Charlie! Josh! Stop it!' said Mum wearily.
'Look, it's choc ices for pudding. You can have
one each, but *only* if you stop arguing and *only* if
you go and eat them in the sitting room.'

Three seconds later the kitchen was peaceful
again.

'Evie, love,' said Mum. 'Are you feeling OK?'

'Yes, thanks,' mumbled Evie, though she wasn't, of course. She was missing Hannah dreadfully, and her ballet class, and her familiar old bedroom with the glittery wallpaper, and . . . well, everything. It was just that she couldn't say so. Mum had so much work to do and Dad was busy starting his new business. If she said she hated school and had no friends, they'd worry even more!

'Well, Dad and I were thinking how hard it is settling into a new place, and we had an idea. Are you doing anything on Saturday morning?'

Evie shook her head slowly, wondering what was coming.

'Have you heard of Mrs Swann?' Mum asked.

'I don't think so,' said Evie.

'Well, she's given you an invitation,' said Dad, with a smile.

'Me?' said Evie, feeling excited. 'What for?'

'Can't you guess?' asked Mum.

Evie shook her head frantically. 'No! Just tell me! What is it?'

'You are invited,' said Mum, pushing a card slowly across the table, 'to The Malkova Dance Academy!'

Evie held the invitation like it was Mum's favourite ornament. It was written on a lilac card

in curly writing, but Evie couldn't read a word:
her eyes were too blurred by happy tears. She ran
round the table and hugged Mum. Then she
hugged Dad. Then she whirled around the
kitchen humming her favourite bit from the
Dance of the Sugar Plum Fairy.

'Before you get too excited,' said Dad,
'remember, it's only a visit. You'll have to pass an
audition to get in.'

Suddenly, Josh burst through the door begging
for another choc ice. Evie felt so happy she
rushed over and hugged him as well, telling him
the good news.

'I want to join a club, too,' he muttered, shaking
himself free from Evie's embrace.

'Well, I'm sure The Malkova Dance Academy
would like an extra boy,' said Dad with a twinkle
in his eye.

'Dancing with *girls*! No *way*!' Josh yelled,

stomping back to the sitting room and slamming the door.

Later, as Evie helped Mum clear the table, the telephone rang.

'I'll get it,' she said, skipping into the hallway. A moment later she squealed, 'Hannah! You'll never guess! I'm going to ballet class!'

Mum finished tidying the kitchen and made herself a cup of tea. She smiled, pleased to see Evie looking so much better, glad to hear her sounding so happy.

'Only ten more days!' said Evie as they planned her birthday get-together. 'I can't wait! We'll go bowling and watch *Dance School Crazy* and eat popcorn, just like we did last year. It'll be *brilliant!*'

Chapter Three

Sugar Glum Fairy

Pale sunlight seeped through the curtains as a chorus of noisy twitterings welcomed the dawn. Evie woke suddenly. Saturday! The academy!

Worried in case she had overslept, Evie leaped out of bed and checked the time. It was only six o'clock! She crawled under her duvet again, but couldn't get back to sleep – her mind was fizzing with excitement.

Although Dad had said she wouldn't dance today, Evie couldn't help herself – she just *had* to put on her old dancing gear. Searching under her bed, she dragged out a case that had been hidden there since the move. Rummaging in it like a lucky dip, she quickly found her pink tights and leotard. They had the friendly wood-and-polish smell of her old ballet school, and suddenly Evie felt tears in her eyes again. *Oh, why did we have to leave London?*

After dressing, she stood in front of her wardrobe doors and gripped the handles like a *barre*. Still tearful, she stood poised, took a deep breath and performed a series of *pliés*, bending her knees like a frog.

With a cheerful rat-a-tat-tat the door opened and Dad's smiling face appeared.

'Dressed already?' he said. 'You must be keen!'

'Yes, I was just practising,' said Evie, hurriedly drying her eyes.

'Mum's on duty at the hospital this morning,'
Dad announced. 'So I'll be taking you. We'll leave
about ten o'clock. Don't forget!'

Evie laughed. Forget! How could she!

With her dancing gear on beneath her coat, they
drove into town and parked in the high street. Dad
led Evie down a passage between a florist shop
and a bakery. The mingled scents of cut flowers
and fresh bread hung in the air, seeming to Evie
like a curtain between the sadness of the move
from London and the promise of dancing once
again.

They came to a paved yard and there, above an
arched doorway, Evie saw the sign: The Malkova
Dance Academy! The faint tinkling of a piano and
a muffled voice calling '*Jeté! Jeté!*' carried across the
yard. Evie trembled with excitement.

'Hello?' called Dad, pushing open the heavy wooden doors and stepping inside.

From a side room appeared a lady with blonde hair combed back into a tight bun. Evie stared. She looked so pretty!

'Hello, I'm Miss Connie,' the lady said with a smile. 'And you must be Evie.'

Evie nodded, looking very serious as they shook hands.

'There's a class on at the moment,' said Miss Connie, 'so let me take your coat and then you can watch the lesson. How does that sound?'

'Wonderful!' whispered Evie, looking all around. The academy was more perfect than she could have dreamed.

Dad said goodbye, then Miss Connie took Evie to the studio. They crossed the wide floor and Evie felt delighted when Beth, who she recognised from school, gave her a tiny finger-wave.

A man with round glasses and hair like a mad professor was playing the *Dance of the Sugar Plum Fairy* as a slender girl with sleek blonde hair performed a beautiful solo. Evie felt a thrill tingle all the way to her toes and couldn't help but dance a few steps across the room: she *loved* that music. Miss Connie noticed and smiled.

'Mr Jacobs!' she called. The music stopped and everyone looked up. 'This is Evie Denham. A fairy tells me she knows this dance. Perhaps she could try a few steps with Lottie?'

Miss Connie gave an encouraging wink, and Evie stepped forwards nervously. The music started, Evie took two steps . . . and stumbled. Lottie's mouth twitched in an ugly sneer.

Feeling terrible, Evie composed herself again and the music began again. Soon it whisked her away, each note carrying her into a graceful glide or lifting her gently to a dainty skip, until she felt nothing but the dance. When the music stopped everyone clapped wildly, Beth loudest of all. Evie bowed timidly and gave Lottie a friendly smile.

Lottie glowered back with a sour pout, hating Evie for stealing the limelight.

Beth, who always felt annoyed at Lottie's 'I'm best' attitude, raced up with her friends Jessica and Lauren and clapped Evie on the back. 'Well done,' she said. 'You were *brilliant!*' Evie thought it was the

happiest moment she'd had since moving to
Crossacre.

* *ᵗ* * ᵗ *ᵗ* * * *

Soon it was time to go, and Evie went into the
cloakroom to fetch her coat. Lottie and her
scowling friends Grace and Olivia stood by the
pegs.

'Excuse me,' said Evie. 'Could I get my coat?'

'Oh, Little Miss Brilliant wants her coat,'
whispered Lottie. 'Should we let her?'

'Not if it came from the same jumble sale as her
leotard,' said Olivia.

'After all, we don't want her letting the academy
down,' added Grace.

Evie burst into tears and ran outside, leaving her
coat behind. *This was the first nice day I've had since we
moved*, she thought. *Why did they have to spoil it?*

Chapter Four

A Birthday Gift

Evie sat on Mum and Dad's bed in her fleecy pink pyjamas. Dad sipped his coffee and slumped back on the pillow, while Charlie and Josh wrestled on the floor.

'Quiet now, boys!' said Mum.

'Awww, do we have to?' said Josh automatically.

'Yes!' mumbled Dad.

'Here you are, Evie, love,' said Mum fondly, and gave Evie a pile of envelopes. 'Happy birthday!'

Evie tore open her cards, laughing at Charlie's cartoon of a ballerina footballer. She kept jigging with excitement, but it wasn't because it was her birthday – it was because, for the first time since they'd moved, Hannah was coming to visit!

Yesterday, in town buying popcorn and the DVD, they'd met Miss Connie who said dance was cancelled this week. Evie had felt a little disappointed, but didn't mind too much – it meant she'd have more time with Hannah!

Evie had just opened Josh's card, a picture of a dancing potato, when the telephone rang. Mum reached for the receiver.

'Oh, what a shame . . .' Evie heard her say. 'Yes, we quite understand . . . Well, do give her our love.'

Mum replaced the receiver and reached for

Evie's hand. 'I'm terribly sorry, love, but –'

'What?' said Evie anxiously.

'That was Mrs Saunders. Hannah can't come today. She's caught chickenpox.'

With tears filling her eyes yet again, Evie ran to her room and flung herself on to the bed. *Everything's gone wrong and I don't have any friends!* she despaired. Then scrunching up her eyes, she whispered, 'I really, really wish, just for my birthday, that I could have a *real* friend.'

A little later, Dad popped his head round the door.

'Evie, sweetheart,' he said. 'Would you like to go to Frankie Joe's Diner for a special birthday tea?'

'Thanks, Dad,' said Evie with a weak smile. 'That would be nice.' Though really, she didn't want to go – somehow, it didn't feel like her birthday any more.

After lunch, Evie was trying to decide which outfit to wear. She had just put on her pink sequinned dress and slung the matching handbag over her shoulder when the doorbell chimed.

'Evie,' Mum called from the kitchen. 'Would you see who that is, please? I'm baking a cake!'

Evie ran to the door and there stood a lady with wispy grey hair and a kind smile on her pretty, bird-like face. A sudden breeze swirled the first fall of autumn leaves in a whirligig dance along the garden path. A scent of strange spices hung in the air.

'Hello,' the lady said. 'I'm Mrs Volkov.'

'Oh, hello,' Evie said politely. 'Did you want Mum?'

'No, Evie, dear. I've come to wish you a happy birthday.'

Evie, who had never seen the lady before, felt confused. *How does she know my name?*

'Ten is a very special age,' the old lady continued, 'and I had an inkling that you, especially, might appreciate this little gift.' She reached inside her shawl, then passed Evie an ancient book with a soft purple cover and crinkly parchment pages. Evie noticed a faint smell of dusty libraries and great-grandmothers. She shook her head – had she really felt a tingle, as soft as a robin's heartbeat, run through her fingers?

'Oh! Thank you,' said Evie.

'Look, here,' Mrs Volkov whispered, pointing to some curly gold writing on the front page.

This diary is for you alone,
A secret you must keep,
Each night, tell me your worries,
And then fall sound asleep.

Then, as the dawn sun wakes you up,
The answer will be here,
Some words to help and guide you,
So you need have no fear.

Evie heard Mum's footsteps coming up the hall
and quickly hugged the diary against her chest.

'Hello, it's Mrs Volkov, isn't it, from number 63?'
said Mum, holding up her flour-covered hands.
'Would you like to come in for a cup of tea?'

'I'm sorry, dear, but I must hurry. Another time,
perhaps?'

'That would be nice,' said Mum. 'See you soon.'

Mrs Volkov said goodbye and shuffled up the
path, leaning on her walking stick. Mum went
back to the kitchen and Evie shut the door. *How
did she know it's my birthday?* she wondered, and
peered through the letterbox to watch Mrs Volkov

totter off. When Mrs Volkov reached the gate she
gave a little wave with her stick, just as if she
knew Evie was looking!

Suddenly, Josh came charging down the stairs,
shouting, 'What are you looking at, nosy?'

Evie spun round, quickly slipping the diary into
her school bag that hung on the coat hook by
the door. She noticed that it was a perfect, snug
fit and felt pleased – it was as though it had been

made especially for her.

'What's that? What've you got?' Josh whined, reaching for the bag and tickling Evie to make her move out of the way.

'Nothing!' Evie said.

'It is! I saw it!'

'Nothing for you, so get off!' said Evie, though she couldn't help but giggle. Then she called out, 'Mum, Josh is being a pest!'

'Josh! Leave Evie alone. Come and give me a hand.'

'Awww, Mu–um. Do I have to?'

Laughing, Evie grabbed the bag and ran to her room: she had to hide the diary before anyone else saw it!

Chapter Five

Evie's Big Day

M rs Volkov's visit and her strange gift put the fun back into Evie's birthday. She spent the whole afternoon trying on different outfits and doing her hair, ready for the meal at Frankie Joe's Diner.

On the drive to Millchester they told silly jokes and laughed at everything so, by the time they clambered from the car, the Denham family was in a daft mood.

Music floated from the open doors of the diner. When Dad heard the tune *Love Me Tender* he danced across the car park doing his Elvis Presley impression and they all ran away crying, 'No, Dad! Pleeeease!'

Inside, the waitress saw Charlie's joke badge, a sad face with the words 'It's My Sister's Birthday!' and sat Evie in the 'Birthday Chair'. Evie cringed, but secretly felt *very* special.

Charlie chomped a gigantic cheeseburger that oozed with sauce and double everything, while Josh almost disappeared behind his enormous pile of chips. Dad munched on some chicken dippers and hummed along to the jukebox, while Mum whispered something about a cake to the waitress.

With all the excitement, Evie *had* to go to the loo. Near the till she saw Beth, Jessica, Lauren and Meera poking different buttons on the ice-cream machine and looking puzzled. She gave a friendly smile and they all waved back.

Passing the kitchen, she overheard the manager say that the ice-cream machine was broken. She'd hardly sat down again when a waiter marched up carrying a gigantic ballerina-shaped cake covered in candles and sparklers. Then a guitar-playing cowboy appeared singing 'Happy Birthday', and everyone in the diner joined in! Blushing crimson, Evie hid behind the ice-cream menu – and suddenly had a fantastic idea!

'Mum,' she said. 'Beth and the others wanted ice cream, but the machine is broken. Could we offer them some birthday cake instead?'

'What a great idea!' said Mum, and asked the waiter for some more chairs. Evie beckoned the girls over, and suddenly they were all having a fantastic party. Dad ordered extra lemonade and even stopped humming!

Of course, the ballerina cake set them all talking about The Malkova Dance Academy . . .

'You danced beautifully last week!' said Jessica.

'And you showed up Lottie!' laughed Lauren. 'It was *hilarious*!'

'You've probably guessed,' said Beth, 'that Lottie Dean just *has* to be the Queen Bee.'

'And,' added Meera, 'she throws a tantrum like a spoiled toddler if she's not!'

They all giggled and went on chatting for ages. Eventually it was time to go and all four girls gave Evie a birthday hug and promised to get together at school on Monday! It couldn't have been a nicer ending to her party tea.

Back home, Evie curled up in bed with a hot-water bottle and was fluffing up her pillow when she remembered the diary! Very gently, she opened the cover. In the soft light of her table lamp she read again the rhyme in curly gold writing, and gasped – two extra verses had appeared, addressed especially to her!

Please, Evie, keep me hidden,
For if anyone finds out,
These words will fade,
and I'll be gone.
Of this there is no doubt.

Then later, when my work is done,
Please don't put me aside.
Pass me on, wish me goodbye,
And someone else I'll guide.

Amazed, Evie turned the page, finding the thick, old-fashioned paper strangely comforting. *This is exactly what I wanted!* she thought, and snatching up her favourite rose-scented gel pen, she began to write.

Dear diary,

Hello, I am Evie! I was ten today! After I woke up, I had the worst morning of my life! Ever! Since we moved, everything has been horrid. Today, Hannah was coming for a birthday sleepover, which was the only good thing — then she was ill!

Anyway, Dad said we could go out for tea. I didn't feel like it, but in the end we went to a really cool diner and I made FOUR new friends! They are sooo nice, I couldn't believe it! And we're going to meet up at school on Monday!

I was really missing dance class so I loved going to The Malkova Dance Academy, but Lottie Dean was so mean I don't think I can go back, even though Beth explained what she's like. Also, in a way, Lottie was right — my dance gear is old and tatty, but it's not my fault. Anyway, I don't think Mum and Dad could afford any new stuff at the moment. I wish I knew what to do.

I really like writing in here, cos there's no one else I can really tell these things to. There's loads more to say, but — yawwwn — I'm falling asleep. So goodnight, diary. The end of my tenth birthday.

As Evie gently closed the book and slid it under her pillow she felt a warm, sleepy wave swoosh over her. For the first time since leaving London, it felt like she was home.

Chapter Six

Who Said That?

Evie woke on Sunday morning to the sound of rain pattering on the window. Drawing her duvet snugly round her shoulders she rolled on her side and tried to catch her dream before it faded away – she had been writing secret tales with a quill pen, scratching the words into an ancient book.

'Oh!' she said, suddenly remembering the

strange diary and feeling very slowly under her pillow. She hoped desperately that there really was a diary, that it hadn't been just a dream.

'Phew!' she breathed, and held the soft velvet cover to her cheek. It felt friendly and warm.

Evie opened it on the first page and wailed, 'Ohhh!' as tears filled her eyes – someone else had written in it! It was her private thing and already they'd spoiled it!

Without even reading the words, she flung it on the bed and stormed on to the landing, screaming, 'Josh, I hate you! Leave my stuff alone and don't you ever, EVER, *EVER* write in my diary again!' She knew it was him – he was the only one who'd seen it!

Josh, still in his Chelsea FC pyjamas, had been watching *TV Toons* in the sitting room. He raced into the hall yelling, 'I never did!' up the stairs at Evie.

Evie screamed back. 'Don't tell lies. You sneaked

into my room. I know!'

Then Dad came out of the kitchen carrying a mug of coffee. 'Evie, love. I don't know what this is all about, but Josh has been here all the time. I was first up and I'm quite sure he's not been into your room.'

Too angry to say sorry, Evie stomped to Charlie's room and banged on the door, shouting, 'Charlie! Have you been in my room?'

When Charlie didn't reply she pushed open his door, but saw that he was heavily asleep.

Muttering to herself, she went back into her room, slamming the door so hard the fluffy fairy lights draped around the door frame fluttered. Then she sat on the edge of her bed with her arms folded tightly, and cried.

When her sobs stopped she glanced at the diary and began to feel a bit silly. She rubbed her eyes on her pyjama sleeve and looked more closely. It was weird, but the new writing looked exactly like the rhyme inside the cover, all in beautiful, old-fashioned curly letters. *Josh or Charlie could never write like that!* she thought, and began to read . . .

Dear Evie,
I'm so glad you have written to me!
Wasn't that a shame about poor

Hannah. I'm sure she was just as disappointed to miss your evening together.

Things don't always happen the way we want, but sometimes you realise afterwards that they happened in the best way.

Just think, if Hannah had come, you wouldn't have met Beth and her friends at the diner. Wouldn't that have been a shame?

Evie nodded her head. She hadn't thought of that, but saw now that it was quite true. Amazed at how the diary could know all this and excited to find out more, she read on . . .

You enjoyed dancing again at The Malkova Dance Academy, didn't you? Although you were out of practice, you danced beautifully! You should be proud of yourself.

Moving to a new place is always difficult, but please don't worry. You're a kind and generous girl, and people like you will always make new friends.

True friendships last forever, and Hannah will always be there. You can't help being apart from her, but I'm sure you'll soon make a whole crowd of new friends.

From your diary with love.

49

Evie's hands trembled as she touched the gold writing with the tips of her fingers, hardly able to believe the words were real. Her head felt swimmy like it did when she had the flu, but in a happy way.

Hearing Mum call her for breakfast, Evie slid the diary under her pillow and went downstairs, trying desperately to guess who had written in it.

'Charlie, have you been in my room?' she asked, trying to appear as casual as possible while chewing a piece of toast.

'No! Why?' said Charlie a little grumpily because Dad had woken him up when he'd wanted a lie-in. Evie didn't answer.

'Josh,' she said. 'Have you got a gold pen in your pencil case?'

Josh shook his head sulkily, still fed up with Evie for shouting at him earlier.

'Why d'you want to know, anyway?' said Charlie.

'Because,' muttered Josh, 'she said I'd written in her diary!'

'Diary?' said Charlie. 'Give it here, then. Let's see what I'm supposed to have done.'

'Er, don't worry. It's nothing,' said Evie quickly, remembering the rhyme from the front of the book:

. . . For if anyone finds out,
These words will fade,
and I'll be gone . . .

She *couldn't* risk giving away the secret!

Chapter Seven

Lottie Trouble

On Monday, Evie woke up fifteen minutes earlier than usual.

The night before she'd told her diary how worried she felt about going to school. What if Beth and the others didn't want her to join them after all? What if she couldn't remember how to do the sums in maths?

Had it replied? With her heart thumping she

pulled it from under her pillow and opened the soft purple cover.

Dear Evie,

Please don't worry. Fitting in at a new school is scary for everyone!

Imagine, it is rather like wearing a new pair of shoes — at first they seem strange and different, but keep wearing them and soon they're perfectly comfortable.

Just think, everyone was new here once and everyone in the world, even the Queen, started out knowing nothing at all!

Evie smiled – she hadn't thought of that . . .

Remember to pay attention and do your very best, and soon everything will be OK.

Though her heart was racing, Evie tried to do as her diary said and strode boldly into school.

Then, as she came into the playground, Beth ran towards her, closely followed by Meera, Lauren and Jessica.

'Evie!' Beth said breathlessly. 'Your party was brilliant!'

'Really fab!' added Lauren.

Evie felt a little overwhelmed – they all seemed so excited.

'Look what we've got you!' said Jessica, as Meera handed Evie a home-made birthday card showing a fantastic cake piled high with rainbow sprinkles, chocolate buttons and creamy whirls.

'Sorry it's late,' said Meera, 'but we didn't know it was your birthday till Saturday!'

'Meera drew it,' said Beth. 'Isn't she brilliant?'

Evie trembled with joy. She opened the card and saw that they had signed it 'From the Crew!'

'I love it!' she squealed. 'I'll put it on my pinboard to remind me of that fabulous party!'

All day Evie felt as though she was floating – at last she had found some friends . . . and back home, under her pillow, she had one *very* special friend.

Even when she got lost taking the register to the office, she didn't get flustered. *Everyone was new here once*, she thought – remembering what her diary had said – and asked a teaching assistant for directions!

Evie came out of school chatting happily with Beth, and saw Mum waiting with Josh at the gate.

As they were walking home, Mum made a sudden announcement.

'Evie, I've a little surprise for you!'

'I want a surprise too!' said Josh, tugging Mrs Denham's sleeve.

'Ah, but it wasn't your birthday on Saturday, was it?' laughed Mum mysteriously, then added, 'Still, we might find you something if you're good.'

They passed the alleyway to The Malkova Dance Academy, and then the florist shop.

'Here we are,' said Mum and directed Evie into a small doorway between the florist and the Post Office that Evie hadn't spotted before. Inside was like a fairy grotto, with twinkling lights in the ceiling, glitter on the shelves and tinsel twirled around every rail. Better still were row upon row of leotards and leggings, crossover wraps and ballet shoes, dancing badges and tutus in a

rainbow of different colours. Evie gazed at
everything and whispered, 'It's heaven!'

'This is the academy shop,' said Mum. 'See that
little door at the back? It leads to the studios.
Anyway, Dad and I thought you deserved a new
outfit for your audition next week.'

'Really? Oh, Mum! Thank you!' Evie cried,
hugging her tight. Together they selected the
whole uniform, plus a spare leotard, all in the

academy colours of lilac and white. They even
bought a matching shoe bag!

Mum was paying at the till, Josh was spinning a
postcard rack round at high speed and Evie,
feeling curious, wandered over to peek into the
studio. Someone was having a modern-dance
lesson, and performing skilfully to the music from
Grease. Miss Connie was teaching, then as the
pupil spun round Evie saw it was Lottie Dean.
The moment the music stopped Lottie came
stomping towards her!

Evie backed into the shop and pretended she
was looking at some ribbons. Lottie barged in
and smiled sweetly at Mrs Denham, who was
chatting to the lady at the till.

Then she pushed Evie into a changing room
and, pointing her finger at Evie's face, hissed, 'I

don't know who you think you are, turning up here and trying to impress everyone, but it won't work with me! This is *my* lesson with Miss Connie, so I don't want you poking your nose in like you did the other Saturday.'

'But –'

'If I were you,' said Lottie, almost spitting the words, 'I wouldn't bother buying any new gear, and I wouldn't bother coming for an audition. We don't want people like you in this school.'

'I only –' whispered Evie.

'Listen!' said Lottie. 'If by some freak chance you do get in, I personally guarantee that you'll find it *totally* unbearable!'

Chapter Eight

Brother Cool

Evie could hardly breathe. Her hands shook and her legs wobbled. Feeling sick, she wished she could hide in her room or, even better, run home to London and never come back!

Mum, who was busy putting her purse away and trying to stop Josh from tugging her hand, hadn't heard a thing.

'Time to go, Evie,' she called, picking up the shopping bags and saying goodbye to the lady at the counter.

Walking home, Evie felt desperate. How could she explain that she didn't want to go to the audition? – Mum had just spent all that money on her new gear! She loved Miss Connie and the academy and *so* wanted to dance again, but how could she with Lottie there? Her thoughts whirled round like clothes in a tumble dryer. *Oh, what should I do? I wish I had someone to talk to.* She felt so upset she didn't even notice that Josh wasn't pestering her.

As soon as they got in, Mum put the kettle on for a cup of tea. She seemed ever so pleased to have bought Evie's new dance gear, which made Evie feel even worse – she really *had* to speak to someone! Then she had an idea.

'Mum, could I phone Hannah, please?'

'Of course you can,' said Mum as she rinsed the teapot.

Evie ran into the hall, shutting the door behind her. She knew the number by heart and dialled quickly. Hannah's mum answered the call.

'Hello, Mrs Saunders,' Evie said. 'Can I speak to Hannah, please?'

'Evie? I'm sorry, pet, but she's gone out for a walk with her friend Alice.'

'Oh . . .' said Evie quietly. She remembered Alice: they had never got on very well, and she hadn't thought Hannah liked her at all. Now the two of them were friends! *How could Hannah do that?* thought Evie. It seemed like even her best friend was forgetting her . . .

'Are you still there, Evie?' came Mrs Saunders' voice from the phone. 'Shall I get Hannah to call when she's back?'

'No, thanks,' Evie said sadly and gently put the phone down.

Usually when she had some new clothes Evie would rush to her room to try them on. Now though, after hearing about Hannah, she left the shopping bags in a heap on the hall floor and went to watch TV.

Mum put her head round the sitting-room door. 'Evie, love. It's nearly six o'clock and Charlie's still at the skatepark in the rec. Would you pop over and tell him it's time for tea?'

Evie nodded and got up slowly, not in the mood for doing anything. Feeling chilly, she slipped on an old coat, then wandered up the road with her head down and hands in her pockets.

Crossing the rec, which was still wet from Sunday's rain, her shoes got muddy and she felt really miserable: she couldn't stop thinking about what Lottie had said.

Reaching the skatepark, she saw Charlie whizzing down the high ramp and doing a series of amazing glides and flips. A crowd of younger boys sat around on their BMX bikes calling 'Yaayyy!' with each brilliant move. Evie wished she could be really good at something – maybe then she'd be popular too!

Feeling too shy to walk out in front of all those boys, she waited a little way back. She recognised a few of them from school, including Anthony and Joseph: if they saw her they'd be sure to make some joke about her coat and repeat it at school the next day.

Charlie came to the end of his turn and skidded to a halt. Spotting Evie, he grabbed his skateboard and jogged over to her.

'Hey, Evie,' he said warmly, and put his arm round her shoulder. 'There's no need to look so

worried! What's up?'

'Mum says it's teatime,' Evie whispered.

'Gosh, I hadn't realised how long I'd been,' he said, and turning to the crowd he waved his board and shouted, 'See you tomorrow!'

Evie noticed Anthony point at her and say something to Joseph, who nodded – they had twigged that she was Charlie's little sister!

For the first time since Lottie had been mean, Evie smiled to herself. *At least I might be more popular with them now, and maybe they won't tease me so much.*

Evie slithered back across the rec, grateful to Charlie for catching her when she almost fell, and even more so for being nice to her.

'You're a bit quiet today,' he said.

Evie wondered if she could tell him about Lottie, but wasn't sure if he would even understand: he was a boy, after all! Anyway, how could he stop Lottie when he didn't go to dance class?

Evie stamped on the pavement to get the mud off her shoes. She'd made a decision – she would wait until bedtime, then tell her diary all about the Lottie Problem!

Chapter Nine

Hideaway

Dear Evie,

 Thank you for writing to me again. I am so sorry to hear about your trouble with Lottie Dean. I do wonder if she's a girl who needs a friend too. Perhaps she thinks that the only way to be popular is to win at everything.

I am sure you know that isn't true — real friends will like you just as you are.

Anyway, dear, you have to be brave. So hold your head up high, go to your audition and do your best. You must never let anyone else (not even Lottie!) stop you from doing what your heart tells you to do, and I'm certain it's telling you to dance!

From your diary with love.

Still feeling puzzled, Evie closed the book. Until yesterday the diary had been perfect, always giving just the right advice.

Now though, she wasn't sure. For one thing, she

knew she couldn't face that audition. Lottie would be there looking daggers at her. Then, what if she did pass? How could she go to the academy knowing Lottie would try to spoil everything?

Perhaps the diary didn't understand after all. Evie knew she wasn't strong enough to stand up against Lottie – whatever the diary said. She slipped it back under her pillow and got ready for school, wondering how to tell Mum that she wouldn't be needing her new dance gear.

School didn't go too badly that day or the next. She hung around with the 'Crew' and joined in the skipping. Anthony and Joseph were still blowing her kisses, but Evie thought they were trying to impress rather than embarrass her! Then, best of all, Beth invited her to tea! *At last*, thought Evie happily, *I've found a real friend.*

The next day at break, Jessica and Meera hurried over to tell Evie what had happened at

jazz dance the previous evening.

'Listen,' said Meera excitedly. 'Snotty Lottie was just doing a really easy sidestep, but messed up.'

'And then,' added Jessica, 'Miss Connie said, "You can do better than that, Lottie. Remember how Evie did it last Saturday and try to follow her style."'

Evie opened her mouth and shut it again, unable to believe what they were saying.

'You should've seen Lottie's face,' said Meera. 'She looked like she'd eaten a slug!'

'She was *so* cross!' Jessica continued. 'She gave us a message for you: "*Totally* unbearable." She said you'd understand.'

'What did she mean?' asked Meera.

Evie nearly burst into tears. 'I've got to go,' she spluttered, and hurried to the toilets, where she locked herself in a cubicle and sobbed.

For the next two days, she avoided everyone, hiding in the library at lunchtimes and keeping her head down in lessons.

As soon as the bell went for the end of school on Friday, she grabbed her bag and scurried off before anyone got a chance to stop her.

With school over for the week, she was feeling a little better as she reached her own road. She was almost home when a swirl of leaves skittered across the pavement. Looking up, Evie saw Mrs Volkov standing by her gate, waiting for someone.

'Hello, Evie,' she said with a kind smile.

That's lucky! Evie thought. *Now I can find out about the diary.* She had been desperate to ask questions like *Where did it come from?* and *How does it write while I'm asleep?* but, now that she had the chance, she felt flustered and couldn't think what to say.

'I'm so glad that the diary has chosen to talk to you,' Mrs Volkov continued. 'I felt sure it would – you seemed just the right kind of girl.'

'Er . . . thank you,' said Evie.

'It is wonderful, isn't it?' said Mrs Volkov with a far-away look in her eyes.

'Mmm,' nodded Evie, still too shy to speak.

'Over the years that diary has helped many, many girls just like you. It's a true friend. You will remember to keep it safe, won't you?'

'Yes,' Evie nodded, and Mrs Volkov turned and tottered slowly up her path. 'Oh, Evie!' she called, without looking back. 'Good luck for the weekend!' Then she slipped inside and gently closed her door.

Evie stared after her, wondering, *Had she been waiting especially for me? And why did she think I needed luck for the weekend?*

After tea, Evie gave a big yawn and said she

wanted an early night. As soon as she was in bed she opened the diary and started writing.

Dear diary,

Sorry I haven't written for a few days. I've felt so mixed up and muddled I didn't know what to do.

I love ballet so much I want to dance forever! I absolutely love The Malkova Dance Academy and Mum and Dad have been so kind taking me to class and buying my lovely new ballet clothes. If I don't do the audition, they'll be really sad.

But I can't do it, really I can't! Lottie Dean is so horrid, she'll make everyone hate me. I wish I knew what to do.

Evie snuggled under her duvet, feeling comforted at last to have shared her worries. Then, with her hand resting on the soft, velvet cover of her amazing friend under her pillow, she fell asleep.

Chapter Ten

Last Words

Early next morning, Evie woke to the rustling of leaves in the trees by her window. She wondered if a storm was coming and drew back her curtain. A dazzle of sunshine burst in – it was a beautiful day!

Suddenly a sick feeling like she had on the school coach gripped her tummy. Audition! She had to tell Mum and Dad that she couldn't go!

Then she remembered the diary. Snatching it up, she turned quickly to the last entry and breathed a giant sigh of relief – it had answered!

Dear Evie,

I'm sorry to hear that you're scared, but you must be brave. Did you know that if you run away from your shadow, it will always follow you? But if you stop, your shadow will stop too.

You truly want to dance, Evie. So please, although you feel anxious, imagine your fear of Lottie is like a shadow: don't run away. Be bold and follow your heart, and I'm sure you will be great.

Good luck!
From your diary with love.

Evie's hands trembled. She'd hoped the diary would give her a different, easier answer.

'Scrambled eggs for sleepyheads,' Mum called up the stairs.

Evie sat at the table, looking pale, as Mum dished up. 'Ready for the big day, love?'

'I think so,' Evie nodded bravely, her heart thumping so loudly she was sure Mum would hear.

'Good morning,' mumbled Josh, Charlie and Dad as they shuffled in with tousled hair and bleary eyes. Charlie rested his head on the table – he *never* got up this early on a Saturday!

Suddenly Evie realised; they were all coming to support her, and she understood that the diary was right – she mustn't run away from Lottie. She *would* do the audition!

After breakfast she raced upstairs and put on her new ballet uniform. Loving the pretty lilac colour and the softness of her wrap, she gave a twirl in front of her mirror.

'Evie!' Dad called. 'Time to go.'

They all piled into the car. Then, just as Dad started the engine, Evie shouted, 'Stop! I've left my bag behind!' As she raced back up the path, she thought she saw a shadow flit across Mrs Volkov's window and smiled, remembering her wish – *Good luck for the weekend!*

Though it felt like she'd eaten a whole swarm of butterflies, Evie walked boldly into the studio. She sat on the bench without looking at the other dancers, and especially not at Lottie.

After what seemed like forever, Miss Connie called her name. Evie took a deep breath and handed the piano music to Mr Jacobs.

'Thanks,' he nodded, and his wispy hair flopped over his eyes. He began to play the haunting music from *Dance of the Sugar Plum Fairy* and Evie danced from her heart, gracefully, beautifully, wonderfully – and when the music ended she finished holding a perfect *arabesque*.

Then Mr Jacobs played Evie's modern variation. She twirled and sidestepped through the piece without a single mistake, finishing with her arms outstretched and her head lifted to the right – straight at Lottie!

Miss Connie walked up to Evie and took her hand.

'Evie, your dances were exquisite. We would be delighted to offer you a place at The Malkova Dance Academy.'

Everyone but Lottie clapped and cheered. Mum, Dad, Charlie and Josh rushed to hug her. Evie's eyes filled with joyful tears and she

squeezed Mum extra tight.

'When you've got changed,' said Dad, 'we'll all go to the tea shop for a celebration!'

Evie felt she was floating to the changing room but, as she reached for her bag, Lottie, Grace and Olivia stepped out from behind the coats.

'You should've learned to dance before you came here,' said Lottie.

'Yeah,' said Olivia. 'They only let you in so's not to hurt your feelings!'

'You call that a *pirouette*?' added Grace.

'More like an omelette!' laughed Olivia.

Then Lottie scowled. 'So, *Evie*, what are you going to do now? Try to be teacher's pet?'

Suddenly, from behind Evie, a cross voice answered.

'Lottie! Girls! I'm ashamed of you!'

Evie spun round – it was Miss Connie, with Beth and the Crew!

'The Malkova Dance Academy welcomes *all* students,' Miss Connie continued. 'If this happens again I shall inform your parents. Understand?'

Turning scarlet, Lottie nodded and flounced out of the room, closely followed by Grace and Olivia.

'Don't listen to their lies,' said Beth, giving Evie a hug.

'She's just jealous cos you danced so well,' said Meera.

'And if she tries any more tricks, she'll have us to deal with!' added Lauren.

'Thanks, everyone,' said Evie. 'I *so* appreciate you rescuing me, but how did you know to fetch Miss Connie?'

Jessica pointed at a little boy in a Chelsea football shirt, who was leaning on the wall outside the changing room. 'He warned us.'

'Josh?' said Evie, and ran to him. 'Josh! What happened?'

'You know in the glittery shop when that girl was horrid to you? Well, I heard!' Josh explained. 'Just now, I saw her go in here before you and I thought I'd better tell someone.'

'Josh, you're the most brilliant annoying little brother ever!' said Evie, and kissed him on the cheek.

'Ugh!' he said, wiping it off, and everyone laughed.

Evie changed, then waved goodbye to all her new friends. Then she stepped through the door into dazzling sunlight, giving her bag a gentle tap: inside was a special *secret* friend – one she felt sure had brought her extra luck today.

'Thank you!' she whispered, as she walked back to the car. 'I'll never doubt you again.'

Dancing Diva

Here are some ballet positions you'll need to know if you want to become a prima ballerina!

First Position

Keep your legs together and feet turned out (from the hips, not the knees or you'll hurt your joints). You should stand straight, all the way from your legs to your head.

Second Position

Now move your feet apart by about one and a half times the length of your foot, again, keeping your legs straight.

Third Position

Bring your feet back together, then place the heel of one foot so it fits into the hollow of your other foot.

Fourth Position

Put your feet as they were in third position, but place one foot about 30 centimetres in front of the other foot.

Fifth Position

Do this position gradually from third position, moving the heel of one foot against the big toe joint of the other. Again be careful not to strain your joints.

Find more cool ballet moves in the next From Your Diary With Love book.

Who's Your Dancing Friend?

1. You love to spend your Saturdays...

a. Shopping for pretty tutus
b. Making up dance moves to your fave pop song
c. Being the centre of attention!

2. The best thing about you is your...

a. Friendliness
b. Sense of humour
c. Diva attitude!

3. Dancing is all about...

a. Being pretty
b. Expressing yourself
c. Everyone watching you!

5. At a sleepover, what do you love most?

a. Watching musicals
b. Gossiping with your friends
c. Showing your friends your latest cool dance moves!

4. Your fave dancing music is:

a. The *Sleeping Beauty* soundtrack
b. 'Breaking Free' from High School Musical
c. Anything in the charts

6. What do you want to be in the future?

a. A prima ballerina!
b. A pop star!
c. An actress!

Your dancing friend is Evie! You both love ballet, best friends and wearing the prettiest tutus and tiaras! Your favourite dance is ballet, so you can show off your perfect *pliés* and graceful *glissades*!

You'd love to dance with Beth! You both enjoy jazz, joking around and having fun with your friends! You love modern dance so you can do all the latest moves in the funkiest fashions around!

Your dancing diva is Meera! You both love any dancing that gets you on stage so you can be the centre of attention! Tap, jazz and ballet are all perfect for making everyone see how totally talented you are!

Modern Miss

Dancing Diva

Ballet Babe

Friendship Fun

Make your friend feel fab by making her this super-cute bracelet!

What you need:

- 3 different colours of ribbon, they should be quite thin and all the same lenth (about 25 centimetres)
- Pretty beads

What to do:

1. Start by making a small, loose knot in the end of the ribbons, to hold them together. Make sure they are all the same length and leave about 4 centimetres free after the knot

2. Now, plait the longer part of the ribbon just like you'd plait your friend's hair

3. To make the bracelet super-special you could add some pretty beads to the plaits as you go

4. Keep going until the bracelet fits round your wrist with about 4 centimetres left at the end. Tie another knot to hold it together

5. Try out the bracelet by putting it round your wrist and tying the two ends into a big bow

6. Once you're happy with it, why not make a matching one for yourself?

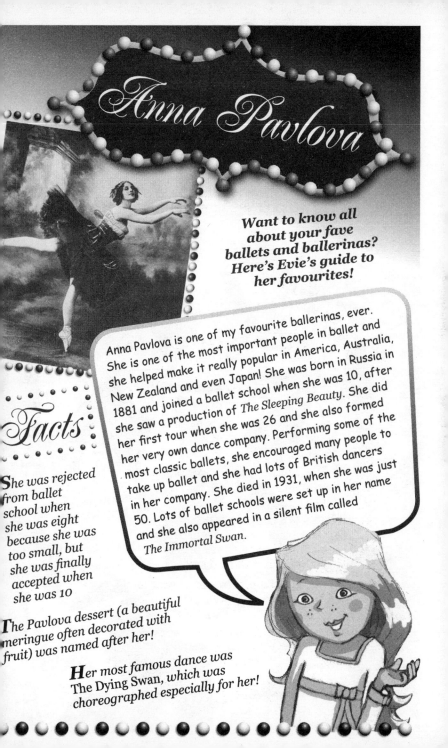

Anna Pavlova

Want to know all about your fave ballets and ballerinas? Here's Evie's guide to her favourites!

Anna Pavlova is one of my favourite ballerinas, ever. She is one of the most important people in ballet and she helped make it really popular in America, Australia, New Zealand and even Japan! She was born in Russia in 1881 and joined a ballet school when she was 10, after she saw a production of *The Sleeping Beauty*. She did her first tour when she was 26 and she also formed her very own dance company. Performing some of the most classic ballets, she encouraged many people to take up ballet and she had lots of British dancers in her company. She died in 1931, when she was just 50. Lots of ballet schools were set up in her name and she also appeared in a silent film called *The Immortal Swan*.

Facts

She was rejected from ballet school when she was eight because she was too small, but she was finally accepted when she was 10

The Pavlova dessert (a beautiful meringue often decorated with fruit) was named after her!

Her most famous dance was The Dying Swan, which was choreographed especially for her!

Memory Magic

How much can you remember from the story? Test your knowledge here and see how you score!

1
Who gives Evie the diary?
a. Mrs Denham
b. Mrs Volkov
c. Mrs Osbourne

2
What is the name of the dancing school?
a. Megabucks Dance School
b. Dancing Divas
c. The Malkova Dance Academy

3
What's Evie's brother called?
a. Charlie
b. Chris
c. Carlos

4
Who thinks she's the academy's star pupil?
a. Beth
b. Lottie
c. Meera

5
What is the name of Evie's old best friend?
a. Hannah
b. Hayley
c. Harriet

6
What's the name of the restaurant where Evie goes for her birthday?
a. Billy Jean's
b. Frankie Joe's
c. Curly Sue's

Answers
1b; 2c; 3a;
4b; 5a; 6b

Can't wait for the next book in the
series? Here's a sneak preview of

From Your Diary with Love

Don't Do Disco

Chapter One

A Star Is Bored

'Poor Jess! Missing ballet to do extra maths,' whispered Evie as she held her arms like a halo above her head. 'It's *so* unfair!'

Miss Connie clapped. 'OK, class. Time to warm down. Breathe out slowly and gently lower your arms.'

'And on a Saturday, too!' said Meera quietly.

'Yes,' murmured Beth. 'It's loads more fun

when we're all here.'

'Well done, everyone!' Miss Connie said. 'Now don't forget – jazz and modern for Wednesday's class.'

A soft patter of ballet shoes scurried across the studio floor to the changing room. Leading the way in a great rush was Matt Shanklin. He had an anxious look on his face and kept pushing his hair out of his eyes.

'Matt!' called Miss Connie. 'Lottie needs a partner to practise her duet. Would you mind staying behind for a few minutes?'

Matt let out a groan and Evie saw his face fall with disappointment. The last thing in the *world* that he wanted to do was stay behind for extra ballet. There were so many better things to be doing on Saturday morning, like lounging on the sofa watching TV!

'Sorry, Miss Connie,' he called, running even

faster. 'I can't today. My mum's waiting for me.'
He reached the boys' changing room but, just as
he stretched out his hand to open the door,
Mrs Shanklin's shrill voice cried out.

'Do stay and dance, Matty, darling! There's no
hurry. I could wait all day if necessary!'

Evie saw Matt falter and his body sag like a
party balloon that had lost its air; he shrugged

and shuffled slowly back on to the dance floor.

The same thing happened every week, but Matt never managed to avoid it.

Two years ago, Mrs Shanklin had watched a DVD and seen Billy Elliot dance his way to fame and glory: from that moment she knew that her brilliant Matty was going to be a star!

First she took him to the hairdresser for a Billy Elliot hairstyle, and then to The Malkova Dance Academy for ballet lessons.

Miss Connie was thrilled to have a boy in her class at last, and Matt found himself playing the male lead in every performance.

Mrs Shanklin thought this *proved* his brilliance! She attended every performance, cheering and clapping more than any other parent. Sometimes she even threw Matt flowers.

'May I stay and watch?' said Mrs Shanklin eagerly and, without waiting for an answer, sat on the bench.

'Poor Matt,' whispered Evie to Beth. 'Maybe he should swap with Jess – he looks like he'd *rather* be doing extra maths!'

Lottie was working for another certificate. Determined to be the best dancer in the academy, she was taking the practice *very* seriously.

Evie, Beth, Meera and Lauren thought it might be interesting and hung back to watch.

'Matt,' said Miss Connie, 'please curl your left arm above your head.'

Matt did as instructed.

'Now bend your right knee . . . just a little more. Very good, Matt.'

'Hurrah! Bravo!' yelled Mrs Shanklin, and clapped loudly.

Lottie pulled a sour face.

Miss Connie raised her eyebrows. 'Now, Lottie. If you would step this way and –'

'Oops!' muttered Matt, losing his balance and stamping on Lottie's foot.

'Owww! Careful, you idiot!' yelled Lottie.

Up jumped Mrs Shanklin. 'Don't you call my Matty names!' she shouted. 'He's a genius!'

'Poor Matt!' said Evie. 'I think we'd better leave.'

Evie spent the afternoon working on her school project – 'The History of Dance in Ancient Rome'. As she worked, she kept thinking of Matt and wondered why he looked so bothered when Miss Connie called him back.

In bed that night, snug in her pyjamas, Evie switched on her bedside lamp. She reached under her pillow and slid out the very special book with a cover of soft purple velvet – her amazing diary. She would write to it like a friend, sharing her thoughts and worries. Sometimes, when she really didn't know *what* to do, it wrote back helpful, understanding advice.

She picked up her favourite rose-scented gel pen and began to write.

Dear diary,

I had a lovely morning with Beth, Lauren and Meera at dance. It was great fun, though we all wished Jess could've been there too.

One thing today made me feel sad, though. Matt Shanklin looked really upset when he had to go back and dance with Lottie.

He's a kind, quiet boy, but his mum is SO loud!

I love Mum and Dad coming to see me dance, but if they made that much fuss I'd be so embarrassed! And he always looks bored cos there aren't any other boys for him to talk to, but I can't help that, cos I'm a girl! I just wish I could help him.

Anyway, then I did some more of my history project and in the evening we watched TV and I had ice cream with about four million sprinkles, because the top fell off the pot as I poured them on! It was brilliant!

Goodbye for now, and goodnight . . .

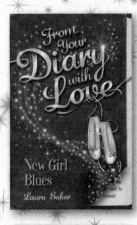

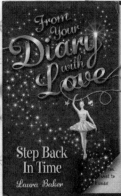

Enid Blyton's ENCHANTED WORLD

Come and join our exciting adventures!

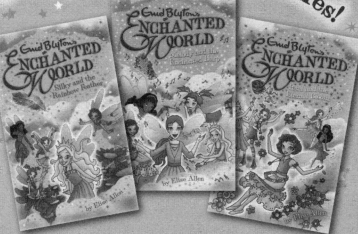

Can Silky and her fairy friends rescue the magical Talismans lost in the Enchanted World before Talon the Troll finds them?

Read our thrilling stories to find out.

In all good bookshops from September 2008

www.blyton.com/enchantedworld